The Ha

and other Strange Tales
of the Oxford Canal

Jane Gordon-Cumming

Jane Gordon-Cumming is the author of the romantic comedy *A Proper Family Christmas*, and a contributor to the OxPens anthologies of Oxford stories: *The Sixpenny Debt* and *The Lost College*. You can read more about her on her website:

janegordoncumming.co.uk

ISBN 978-1-904623-15-1

Published by OxPens

The Haunted Bridge

and other Strange Tales
of the Oxford Canal

Jane Gordon-Cumming

"Stories spookily and splendidly told - with (praise be!) a
map to guide us all." - *Colin Dexter*

Introduction

W hen I wanted to write a ghost story for a competition, I knew exactly where to set it - the derelict quarry at Shipton-on-Cherwell, one of the spookiest places I know. They've broken my heart by surrounding it with a high fence now, so you can no longer climb the secret staircase beside Baker's Lock, and you'll have to take my word for it that it's as unearthly and magical and extraordinary as I describe. I wanted to share my experience of this wonderful place, before they turn it into a housing estate or an eco-town or fill it with unsold cars, or worse, sanitise it into a visitor attraction with steps and nature trails and barricades to stop you getting too close, like poor old Kirtlington Quarry.

And having written 'The Death Trap', I kept thinking of more places and events connected with the Oxford Canal which would make the perfect setting for a ghost story, - the ruined manor at Hampton Gay, the deep lock at Somerton, the Shipton Railway Disaster. In fact, I realised, I could write a whole volume of them.

I have loved the Southern Oxford canal ever since joining my sister Katie and her husband on a cruise from Banbury to Oxford. That was back in the 70s, when the fighter jets still startled one with a sudden deafening roar as they took off from Upper Heyford, and you might still have to operate the old swing railway bridge across the Sheepwash Channel. Katie and Desmond went on to own a pair of hotel boats, and I cadged a trip whenever they had a spare berth. When I married Edwin, I insisted on a canal-based honeymoon, and he became as bitten by the bug as I was. We used to hire from Aynho, and then from College Cruisers, eventually buying one of their boats for our own. Edwin has now converted Worcester to diesel-electric drive, and we can glide through those beautiful wooded cuttings and hear nothing but the birds. In a way these stories are my tribute to the canal.

I should say at once that, although the places and historical background are real, none of these are accounts of genuine sightings. I'm sure there must have been a few, in a place so full of history and tragic stories, but I have not come across them.

I've arranged the stories in geographical order, as one might travel north along the canal from Oxford. Edwin has drawn you a map, so you can see where each story takes place. Like their surroundings, the stories become increasingly spread out as they leave the bustle of Oxford, finally ending in that remote, bleak area of countryside between Napton and Braunston, a 'Landscape of Ghosts' where the past seems so much more real than the present.

Acknowledgements

I have so many people to thank for their support and encouragement.

First of all Chas Jones, a mentor as much as a publisher, who immediately saw the potential of my idea and used his imagination and experience to turn it into the book you have in your hands.

My friends in the Oxford Writers' Group, who not only approved what I'd done, but allowed me to make it something of a companion volume to our successful OxPens anthologies of 'Oxford stories'.

Colin Dexter has been immensely kind, sparing the time to listen to my tales, and going to endless trouble helping me find just the right title for them. The map was his brainwave too.

Alan Burnett took the spooky photo of the haunted railway bridge. The rest are mine.

But none of this could have happened without my helmsman, engineer, cook, draughtsman and travelling companion for better or worse, to whom I dedicate the book.

For Edwin, of course

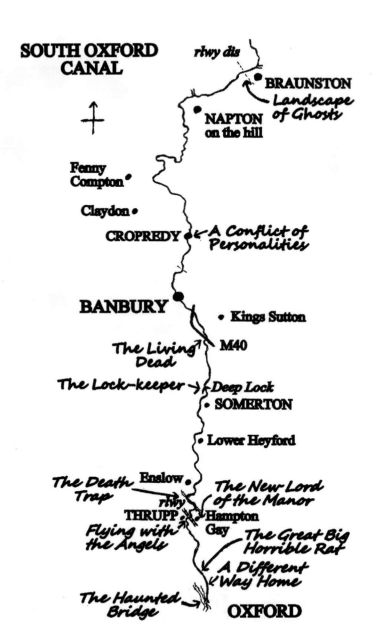

Contents

The Haunted Bridge

The railway bridge over the Sheepwash Channel is haunted. No one knows exactly whose unquiet spirit has chosen to take possession of those gloomy metal girders, but there are plenty of candidates from over the centuries. The monks of Rewley Abbey, angry at their dispossession by Henry VIII; the convicts from the Castle Gaol who were forced to build Louse Lock. Perhaps an incautious young bather at Tumbling Bay still feels the need to lark about, or some homeless victim of alcohol poisoning or hypothermia wants to wreak his revenge on society. Maybe one of those shepherds slipped while washing his sheep in the channel, and was caught for ever more in the treacherous currents where the Four Streams meet.

It would be all very well if the thing confined itself to throwing bricks off the crumbling wall at the end of Abbey Road, or stroking one's hair with a ghostly hand as one passes beneath in a boat, but this sprite has developed a more disturbing line. It senses the fear of each individual who enters its domain, and then takes the most appropriate form.

Suppose your particular phobia is birds. See that pigeon, - the bigger one, with the yellow, watching eye, sitting on the girder in the dark? That's it, waiting to fly out, fluttering in your face, suffocating you with those flappy wings, pecking your vulnerable nose. What about spiders? - Just out of the corner of your eye, scuttling into the shadows by the brickwork, waiting for the chance to extend one of those big hairy tentacles and catch your clothes as you pass by. The nervous walker, hovering to keep his balance on the narrow kerb by the permanent puddle on the towpath, will find a stone suddenly tips up under his feet. In times of flood, beware of trying to wade through to the Thames that way, for you are bound to feel a cold, clutching hand seizing your ankle under the water.

One summer's evening, Darren and his girlfriend Julie were walking along the canal from Jericho, heading for the Botley Road.

"We'll go through here," said Darren, when they came to the Sheepwash Channel. "It's a short cut."

Julie followed him as he turned right and led her across the mill stream. That part is called Snake Island, but luckily Julie wasn't afraid of snakes. She followed him past the battered old swing bridge, left to rot among the brambles, and along beside the windows of the new housing estate, built so disconcertingly close to the footpath. - But then they came to the railway bridge.

"Ooh er," said Julie. "I don't fancy going under there!"

"What d'ya mean? Don't be stupid."

"It looks really spooky."

"Come on, you may have to bend your head a bit. Block your ears if a train goes over," Darren grinned.

"Isn't there another way across?" Julie looked hopefully at the gate next to them, but it was only for railway workers and well padlocked.

"Nah, it's miles round. - Don't be such a girl, Jules," said Darren, who was never afraid of anything, and he took her hand and pulled her down the path after him.

Julie's thing was bats. She could soon see that there were hundreds of them flying in and out of the shadows under the bridge, hunting the evening insects over the water.

"Eek, - *bats*, Darren! You know how I hate bats!"

"I've told you before, they won't touch you. They have this radar thing that stops them bumping into stuff," said Darren, who had once switched onto the Nature channel by mistake. "There's nothing to be afraid of."

But he had reckoned without the spirit. No sooner had Julie stepped into the shadows of the bridge, when a giant bat flew down from one of the beams. It made straight for her hair and entangled itself there, with clingy little hands, and leathery wings, and sharp mousy teeth, and Julie's screams could be heard from Carfax to Cumnor.

"Aren't you scared of *anything*, Daz?" she asked, when he'd eventually calmed her down to a quivering wreck who could just about speak between sobs, and she was trying to pluck up the courage to go on.

"Nah, not me! ...Well, there is one thing I suppose," he admitted with reluctant honesty.

"What? - What is it *you're* scared of?" Julie felt it would help her to know that Darren too had his vulnerabilities.

"Ghosts."

"*Ghosts?*" Julie went off into a peal of hysterical laughter. "I thought you meant something real! How can you possibly be scared of ghosts, Daz? Why, they don't even exist!"

"Yeah, - I suppose not. But still, if there's one thing that does scare me a bit, it's them." He looked at the ground, embarrassed.

When Darren looked up again, he saw a figure. It was standing at the far end of the railway bridge, outlined against the river, - hooded, silent and sinister. As he watched, it began to glide towards them. Darren let out a strangled gasp of terror, and clutched at Julie's arm.

"Okay, no need to pull, I'm coming now," she told him, "so long as there are no more of those bats! It's quite nice this bit of the river, isn't it, once you're through the bridge? And it must be a much quicker way to Botley..."

When you go under the railway bridge over the Sheepwash Channel, be very careful not to show your fear.

A Different Way Home

Alex was walking back from school along the towpath beside the canal. It wasn't the quickest route home, involving a detour quite a long way to the left, but it was a route home, and he was very pleased to have found it. With a bit of luck it just might keep him out of trouble.

So far so good. Nothing more threatening than a mum with a little kiddie in a push-chair, throwing bread at the ducks by the Walton Well bridge. This part of the canal was very quiet, where the gardens of the big North Oxford houses came down to the water, peaceful and golden in the last rays of September sunshine. Round the next bend, and his own bridge would be in sight.

His mother would go up the wall if she knew, - not only that Alex wasn't coming back the way she had carefully shown him, along Walton Street and Kingston Road, but if she had known the reason. It had crossed his mind to tell her, - but not for long. She would want to talk to the teacher at his new school, and Mrs. Heyfield would want to know who the boys were. They would find out he had told on them, and everything would be even worse. Anyway, Alex didn't know their names. He referred to them in his mind as 'the lads'.

It had started as 'laddish' behaviour, - a bit of teasing and shouting. They had seen his mother walking him down that first day, that was the trouble.

"Hey, it's the Milky Bar Kid! No Mummy today, to hold your hand?"

Alex had made a mistake by trying to explain. They'd only just moved here from London. She'd been showing him where the school was...

But that meant the lads heard his voice, so different from theirs. "Ooh, posh boy from London! Why doesn't Daddy pick you up in the Rolls?"

The next day he had tried to walk past without saying anything, but then it was: "Too snobby to talk to us, posh boy?" The day after that, there'd been a bit of jostling, and then someone said "Let's see if he's got any money. You can spare it, can't you, with Daddy being a millionaire?"

And then, on an exploratory walk with his parents on Sunday, they'd come across the bridge. It led to the Meadow, but if you went over it and turned left, you could go right down the canal, where there was another bridge across into Jericho. It was a different way to school, longer, but much safer. Alex had been using this new route all week.

He'd reached the stage now of enjoying the walk. It was much prettier down here than on that busy road. There were birds singing in the willow-trees in the canal-side gardens, and a nice cat who smiled back at him when he paused to click his fingers. He rounded the bend, and the towpath stretched ahead of him quite empty, - and then suddenly, there they were.

They must have come out of the gap in the hedge that led to the recreation ground. In the moment before they saw him, while they were still laughing and shouting and pushing each other about, Alex weighed up his chances. The bridge that would take him home was tantalisingly near, but the group filled the path in between. On his left was a ditch and high wall, guarding the estate behind it like a fortress. To his right, lay the smooth green lane of the canal. If only it were as glassy as it looked! The only option was to run back the way he had come, but they would catch him in seconds. Anyway, it wasn't a good idea to show them fear. In those few seconds Alex resigned himself to the inevitable. If he didn't fight back, and gave them what he had, it shouldn't last long.

They spotted him then, with a crow of delight. "Hey, posh boy! We wondered what had happened to you. Thought you'd try a new way home?" He took a deep breath and carried on towards them.

What made him look round? He was never sure. A sound at his shoulder, perhaps, in that space to his right where no sound should be. He turned, and saw the very thing he might have prayed for, - a bridge across the canal. It was an old-fashioned looking wooden bridge, the kind with arms so you could lift it up and down. Why had he never noticed it before? It rested invitingly against the bank beside him, with its arms in the air on the other side, still trembling slightly, as if someone had just let it down from their garden. ...Funny, though, there didn't seem to be a garden that end. Instead he could see a track leading off in the direction of Kingston Road, - just where he wanted to go.

Alex didn't hesitate more than a second before hurrying across, expecting any moment to feel the bounce of running feet behind him.

But no feet followed. And the shouts he heard were not those of triumphant pursuers about to catch up with their quarry. They were more like cries of fear.

"Bloody hell!"

"Pretty big jump."

"Can he fly, or what?"

He reached the bank, and turned to see what had put that sound into their voices, why they hadn't come after him.

It was probably because the bridge wasn't there. The canal was as quiet and green and glassy as ever, but now it lay between Alex and his pursuers. He was standing in somebody's garden, looking across at his enemies.

"Respect, man." The group moved off, shaking their heads.

As Alex went up the path and let himself out of the garden gate, something told him that after today he would have no more trouble from the lads.

Bridge 241 is now missing from the canal. It was probably demolished when the houses at the north end of Southmoor Road were built in 1882. **Mark Davies & Catherine Robinson:** *Our Canal In Oxford p.16-18 (Towpath Press, 1991).*

The Great Big Horrible Rat

Sandra's husband was a great big horrible rat. She didn't know about reincarnation, so when she murdered him, she didn't expect him to come back as... You've guessed.

One's supposed to improve each time, but Micky hadn't. He was still a great big horrible rat. He lived on that little farm by the lift-bridge in Wolvercote, close to the houseboat he had shared with Sandra. He'd pursue lady rats, and scavenge in the rubbish enclosure, and frighten the boaters, and generally made a nuisance of himself.

His main aim was to bring misery to Sandra, as in his previous life. Sandra, however, was getting on very well without him. His smelly socks and beer cans were no longer cluttering up the *Daisy May*. She could cycle down the towpath to see a film, and not expect a beating when she returned. And she was beginning to make friends with Barry on the *Flying Frog* next door.

Of course Micky hoped that his murder would be discovered and Sandra punished for it, but his lifetime habit of wandering off for periods whenever he felt like it meant that nobody realised he was dead. He didn't go out to work, or visit his mother on Sundays, or attend yoga classes. Nobody noticed Micky was missing from Wolvercote, let alone the world.

He used to visit the place where Sandra had buried his body, in the undergrowth between the towpath and the railway line, but nobody else did. He considered moving some of his bones into a place where they would be discovered and arouse curiosity, - but even to a great big horrible rat there's something a little distasteful about digging one's own remains up and carrying them around Wolvercote. He tried sitting on the spot, hoping people would mistake him for Attractive and Interesting Wildlife and come and investigate, but no one thought he was an otter or a water-vole. Words like 'super rat' were mentioned, and not in a good way.

Then one day, his chance came. Two police officers were walking down the canal, one male and one female. Micky ran out and tried to attract their attention by circling their legs and running back to the place where Micky the Bad Husband had been buried.

But people who find a rat running round their legs don't tend to say: "Oh look, it must be trying to attract our attention to where its previous incarnation was buried after being hit over the head with a whisky bottle!" They tend to say "Vermin". The lady PC jumped two feet in the air - they are only human, and the male used a pejorative expletive.

Sandra came out from Barry's boat to see what all the fuss was about. Her guilty conscience didn't cause her to duck back into the *Flying Frog* when she saw the Police. In fact she'd forgotten she even had a guilty conscience, the crime having been so well justified. The farmer from the small-holding came out with his shot-gun and aimed it at the bushes. Micky fell dead on top of his former incarnation, and nobody bothered to look for his remains.

It will be even harder for him to haunt Sandra and get revenge for his two deaths now. This time Micky has come back as a miserable little louse.

Flying with the Angels

Christmas Eve! Mary Aldridge's heart raced with excitement as the train puffed northwards. Soon she would be seeing her mother and little sisters again. She clutched the small parcels she had for them, - not that she could afford much on a servant girl's wages, but she knew the girls would love the rag dolls from Oxford market, and her mother would treasure the needle-case she had spent the evenings embroidering, up in her attic room.

The carriage was crowded, full of chattering passengers, everyone, like her, excited at the thought of seeing loved ones for Christmas. Mary had managed to get a seat by the window, and she pressed her nose against the glass, glad to be in this safe, warm world on such a cold day. There was the canal she sometimes walked beside on her afternoon off. Smoke rose from the chimney of the cottage beside Duke's Cut, but the lock, which should have been lively with people and horses, was eerily still today, the barges lying motionless, imprisoned in their moorings by the thick ice. This wouldn't be a good Christmas for boatmen's families. How lucky she was to have steady work in the large Banbury Road house, and employers who were kind enough to spare her for the holiday.

Lesley Davenant checked her list again, - at least the second time since the train had left Banbury. Had she forgotten anyone? Too late now. Oh dear, she did hope that computer game was the one Gary had meant. The shop in Castle Quay had said she could change it after Christmas, but it was a long way to come back from Oxford if it turned out she'd bought the wrong thing. Maybe this last minute shopping trip hadn't been a good idea, with such a lot to do for tomorrow. Must remember to get the turkey in from the garden shed, and defrost the cream cheese for the starter. Would everyone be happy with salmon mousse? She had a feeling Alan's sister wasn't very keen on fish, come to think of it. Better make her something else. Christmas was such a stressful time, getting everything right for everybody.

She gazed out at the frozen landscape, trying to dismiss a pervading feeling of unease. It was beautiful, this part of the Cherwell valley, the canal and the river weaving sometimes apart, sometimes together. The scene ahead might have come straight from a Christmas card: Shipton, with its pretty church by the bridge, Hampton Gay church opposite, alone in its deserted fields, and the picturesque ruins of the manor, gaunt among the trees. Why couldn't she just relax and enjoy this lovely view? Anyone else would be looking forward to Christmas Day. There was nothing more she could do, sitting here on a train, and anyway, tomorrow would probably go swimmingly. ...Yet still Lesley couldn't rid herself of the conviction that something terrible was about to happen.

Mary loved being in the train, flying along behind the engine wrapped in a cloud of steam. This must be how the angels felt as they flew across the sky, looking down on all the people below. The train whistled a warning and they rattled over a level crossing. She caught a glimpse of a little hump-backed bridge with a lock beyond, frozen and deserted. A man in a farm cart was waiting for them to go by, on his way to take extra food to those sheep in the fields on the other side of the line. She felt sorry for him, out there in the cold instead of in the nice warm train. Farmers had to tend their stock whatever the weather, poor things.

Damn, what was the hold up? With a slow squeal of brakes, the train had made one of those mysterious stops in the middle of nowhere that trains are prone to. They had ground to a halt in some wretched industrial estate in Kidlington. In growing frustration, Lesley watched the cars shooting past on the main road, and fantasised about leaping out and catching a bus. It could only be about ten minutes to Oxford.

Ah, this must be what they were waiting for. A steam train was approaching on the other line, - a Christmas excursion for railway buffs from Didcot, no doubt. Lesley turned to watch it go past, fascinated in spite of herself, a little surprised that no one else in the carriage seemed interested. What a strange collection of stock they'd put together, - two steam engines, with a funny little old carriage in between, and then a guard's van before the rest of the carriages. It was as if they'd taken up a challenge to use every exhibit in the Railway Museum. This train was stopping too. It drew up beside her, enveloping everything in a great cloud of steam.

Good heavens, they had gone to town! The train itself might look a bit odd, but the carriages were full to bursting, and every passenger was dressed in authentic looking Victorian costume, without a single trendy hair-cut or pair of modern glasses to spoil the illusion. These steam buffs really did like to do things properly. A girl of about fourteen was sitting in the carriage opposite, her cheeks rosy under a wide-brimmed hat, her eyes bright with excitement. Lesley felt a sudden pang of envy for the girl's ability to give herself up to such frank, unadulterated pleasure. This child wasn't weighed down with responsibilities at Christmas. Nothing to do but enjoy her trip on a steam train, and look forward to further delights tomorrow.

Across the crowded carriage Mary could just read the name above the platform: 'Woodstock Road'. That was the station for Kidlington, wasn't it? She didn't know why the express had paused here. The passengers glanced at each other, but no one alighted, and there was certainly no room for anyone else to squeeze in.

Mary turned back to her own window, and saw that another train had drawn up next to theirs. How pretty! Instead of the familiar cream and brown, it was a gay red and silver. They must have done it like that specially for Christmas. The lady in the carriage opposite her seemed very thinly dressed for this cold day. She wore no hat over her dark hair, and her scarf was little more than a flimsy handkerchief knotted round her neck. Yet she didn't look poor. Her face was smooth, more like a lady's than someone who worked for a living, and her lips were coloured an unreal cherry red. Mary pursed her own unadorned lips. She knew what kind of women painted their faces. Nevertheless, there was something about this stranger which claimed her attention. In contrast to the gaily decorated carriage she rode in, the woman wore an anxious frown, as if all the cares of the world were on her shoulders. Why did she look so unhappy on Christmas Eve? As her train began to move away from theirs, Mary gave the sad lady a friendly smile, trying to encourage her to forget her troubles, if only for a day.

Hm, cheeky madam! - Grinning at her in that 'cheer up, it may never happen' way. Christmas *was* going to happen, whether Lesley was ready or not. It wasn't something one could postpone till one was more in the mood. And there was no denying, she couldn't have been less in the mood.

She tried to talk sense into herself, as the train gathered speed. Even if the meal wasn't perfect, and the presents not precisely what everybody wanted, they would probably still have a very nice time. No one else around seemed to have this gloomy attitude to Christmas. Every window in that housing-estate showed cheerful coloured lights and glittering trees. Even that guy trundling over the hump-backed bridge in a tractor had tied a sprig of holly to his cab, poor sod. At least she didn't have a job which involved being outside in the cold every day.

But counting her blessings didn't seem to be doing Lesley any good. As they rumbled over the crossing with the road from the Garden Centre, the feeling of dread became almost overwhelming.

Off again across the fields! It was like a ride at St. Giles's Fair, Mary thought, but one that went on and on. The boatmens' village of Thrupp was eerily quiet, its line of barges waiting for the thaw, its wharf still and silent. There was the little church beside the railway line and the old manor house in the trees beyond, all that was left of the village of Hampton Gay. What kind of Christmas party would they be having in the manor, the lords and ladies?

But Mary didn't envy them. She was superior to the whole of mankind, flying past in her train. Almost she felt they were about to take off into the sky. How wonderful that would be! Soaring up to heaven to go and meet the angels.

...What was happening? For one glorious moment it seemed that her dream had come true. Mary found herself flying through the air, free of the train and the rest of the world. She didn't feel the bang, or the icy water. By the time her carriage sank into the freezing canal, her soul was already with the angels.

Lesley wasn't sure when the oppression began to lift, all she knew was that she suddenly felt a lot better. Perhaps it was the sight of the Oxford ring road ahead, the psychological boundary of home. Didn't the canal down there at Duke's Cut make a lovely winter's scene? - the lock, and its white cottage and the arching brick bridge. They should come up here for their Christmas walk tomorrow. ...Oh come on, it was all going to be fine. Why not relax and look forward to the day, instead of worrying about things that might never happen? That young girl in the other train had the right attitude. Make the most of the moment, and enjoy life while you had the chance.

On 24th December 1874 a train came off the rails at Shipton-on-Cherwell and 34 people lost their lives.

The New Lord of the Manor

Gary couldn't resist a smile of satisfaction as he walked up the field. There it was, his latest purchase, bathed in the evening light. To anyone else, it might be simply an old ruin, but to an acute businessman like Gary it represented Potential. - Look what they'd done with Oxford Prison, after all. If they could turn a jail into a posh hotel, how much more attractive would this old manor house be? Sure, it was a big undertaking, but that castle he'd seen on *Grand Designs* had started out in much the same condition. He wouldn't faff around trying to save bits of the original stonework either, - a pointless waste of time and money, when breeze-blocks and cement would do the job very nicely. It would mean shelling out a bit, but then Gary had got the site at a knock-down price. "After all," he'd told the guy, "there's nothing much I can do with it. Far too many regulations when it comes to a Scheduled Monument. If I take the place off your hands, it'll be for sentimental reasons, and obviously I couldn't pay full whack..."

It was a lovely summer's evening. A bird was tweeting away in a nearby tree, and there were nice flowery smells in the air. Gary wasn't big on nature, but it added to his general feeling of contentment. All this was his now: the ruined manor, the church, and the lumpy field under his feet. He was Lord of the Manor, and had a certificate to prove it. How good that would look framed in the foyer of the new hotel! He must find out if there wasn't a special robe to go with it, something to impress the punters at dinner. Below him the canal ran past the foot of the hill, a winding strip of gold reflecting the sunset. - He could use that, maybe. Canals meant boats, and holiday-makers. What about a little marina, where the arm of the river led off towards the old mill?

Yes, Gary was full of plans.

Not that they'd been very encouraging at the *Boatman's Rest*. He'd only dropped in there to show his face, give the local yokels a sight of their new Lord of the Manor, and pick up any useful information. They were ready enough with information, but it wasn't exactly what Gary had bargained for.

"The Lords of the Manor ain't never been very popular round here," said an old gaffer seated in the corner. "Not since one o'them took it into his head to turn everyone out of their houses so's he could use the land for sheep. Nothing left of the village now, but them lumps and bumps in the field."

"For Christ's sake, that was hundreds of years ago!" Surely even these bumpkins weren't capable of holding a grudge that long?

"T'weren't only that," put in another, nursing a pint which Gary had paid for. "Some say as the Lord of the Manor refused to give any help after that terrible railway accident, - when the train came off by the bridge and all those people were killed."

"Nay, that can't be right. I heard they used the manor house to lay out the bodies in," observed the man beside him, with gruesome relish.

"But you can't deny the house was burnt down not long afterwards," argued the first idiot. "They reckon as how it were the villagers getting their revenge."

"Well I don't know about that," said a young man leaning on the bar, who looked a bit more sensible. "The fire might have been co-incidence. ...What's absolutely certain, though, is that the place is haunted."

"Stands to reason," nodded the girl with him. "All those people dying so suddenly only a few yards away."

"Nonsense!" the old codger rebuked her. "It's them poor villagers, starved out of their homes and livelihoods by sheep. They're the ones doing the haunting."

"There won't be ghosts of any kind in that house by the time I've finished with it," Gary had told them, and outlined his scheme to rebuild the ruined manor as a luxury hotel, with en-suite bathrooms, a gym and a spa.

They listened politely, but didn't seem as impressed as he would have expected.

"You won't be the first to have had ambitious plans for the Manor," the old coffin-dodger told him. "But it's like I said, the place doesn't welcome landlords. No one who's bought it has ever done any good there. ...What happened to that young man who was going to turn it into a theme park, Harry? Never heard any more from him, did we?"

"Nor did anyone else, if the rumours are right," grinned the ghoulish Harry. "Must have changed his mind and skipped the country."

"I'll tell you one thing," said the younger guy, who was clearly out to impress his girlfriend. "I wouldn't go up there at night. Those ruins are really spooky! There's something malevolent about the place, if you ask me." And all the other cretins had nodded, as if he was talking sense.

Gary wasn't bothered by such rubbish, of course. The spookier the better, as far as he was concerned. People liked that kind of thing, didn't they? That's why the old prison had done so well. - Come to think of it, maybe those dimwit yokels had given him an idea. As he climbed the last bit of the hill, Gary examined his investment with newly calculating eyes. Yes, the ruined manor in the gathering dusk did have a sinister appearance. He'd already seen its potential for murder mystery weekends. But what about something more - well - scary? 'Dare you spend a night at the Haunted Manor?' That would look good on a poster. It would be easy enough to lay on ghostly figures, clanking chains, unearthly shrieks. The punters would love it.

Within the shadow of the ruins, it was almost dark. Bats were flittering round the stone mullions of the empty windows, and the jagged outline of the chimney stack made a stark pattern against the purple sky. An owl called from somewhere in the trees above him, an eerie sound indeed for anyone of a less practical turn of mind than Gary.

God, the place certainly was in a state! Huge lumps of ivy draped the walls, twisting into fantastic shapes, lumps with heads and bodies one could almost see as human. - Did that one just move? No, of course not. One of the fronds had lifted in the breeze, that's all. Well, he'd have all this down for a start! Gary flicked it contemptuously. And he doubted if there was much of the structure worth keeping underneath. Better to have the whole thing down and start afresh.

He leaned against the wall and surveyed the view from the arched doorway. The church was rather in the way, but the authorities had made it very clear to Gary that he wouldn't be allowed to pull that down. Never mind, perhaps he could find a use for it. - Ghost evenings, perhaps. Vicars would do anything to get people into a church nowadays.

Christ, this stuff grew quickly! A tendril of ivy had already managed to wrap itself round his arm. Gary yanked at it angrily and succeeding in breaking it off, but meanwhile another had crept round his waist. He tried to pull away, but found himself tripping up instead, caught by the ankles.

This was ridiculous. The faster he got rid of one piece of this damned creeper, the faster more strands seemed to whip out and grab him, pinning him against the wall. - Hell, there was a knife in his pocket, if only he could reach it, but his lower body was already too tightly bound.

He made a desperate flailing movement with his arms, before they were captured as well. There was nothing he could do to stop the ivy engulfing his shoulders, winding round his neck. He opened his mouth to shout, but before he could call for help, the ivy was inside his mouth, creeping down his throat, binding his eyes.

That evening another man-shaped lump of ivy was added to the wall of the old ruined manor.

The Death Trap

The canal holiday had been a mistake. We'd booked it months ago, when being cooped up together in a small boat had seemed a romantic idea. I would enjoy watching birds and identifying wild flowers, while Pete, the engineer, would be in control of a gear-stick and throttle. Perfect. - Except that it was now becoming clear that our chalk and cheese relationship was going nowhere. The novelty of meeting someone so totally unlike ourselves had worn off, to be replaced by increasing irritation. We were both aware that we had come to the end of the road. All it needed was for one of us to be brave enough to start The Conversation.

But meanwhile, here was the holiday booked and paid for. We collected the boat at Oxford, and chugged our way up the canal, both grateful that the noise of the engine made it impossible to talk. I sat in the bow with my binoculars, hopping out to work locks and lift bridges, while Pete hogged the steering. - Okay, I mightn't have been much good at it, but I would have liked the chance to have a go.

It's amazing how quickly the canal can seem remote. One minute you're passing suburban gardens, the next you're deep in the countryside, apparently miles from anywhere. It was while I was holding open a lift-bridge in one of these spots that I first saw it, a cluster of towers on the skyline. Even at this distance they looked forbidding, a patch of eeriness in the peaceful rural landscape.

"What's that?" I asked, as I climbed back on board. "A ruined castle or something?"

"No," Pete grinned in the way I had begun to find patronising. "It's the old cement works."

"Oh."

Nevertheless, I couldn't take my eyes off the place. It seemed to follow us, growing ever nearer, as if it was on the move, not us, twisting into different configurations of dilapidated buildings and a single tall chimney, larger and more sinister with every bend of the canal.

The next lock was a difficult one, made diamond-shaped to accommodate the flow from the river, whose bed we were about to share. Pete condescended to leave me at the tiller, while he worked the complicated paddles and the heavy gate, and tutted when I failed to hold the boat steady in the awkward current.

Beyond was a beautiful winding stretch flanked with bulrushes and yellow irises. Warblers flicked about in the reeds and white-throats sang from the tops of the hawthorn bushes. I couldn't help calling out to Pete in excitement at spotting the straight blue dart of a kingfisher winging down ahead of us. The old works had disappeared behind the hill, and out of my consciousness.

It was when I turned to follow a heron, disturbed by the boat, flapping up over the tree-covered bank to our left, that I realised with a start that the works hadn't disappeared at all. They were so close above our heads that I hadn't seen them, looming high over the canal, gaunt and threatening. I gazed up in a mixture of horror and fascination as we moved into the shadow of one giant structure, its roof a skeleton of rafters and wayward beams. Rooks wheeled in and out of the weed-covered brickwork with their sad, slow wing-beats, crying mournfully of lost souls. Beside it, that great chimney tapered endlessly upwards. I could swear it swayed against the sky.

"It is a bit spooky, isn't it?" admitted the usually insensitive Pete. "Still, I think we'll moor up here for the night."

"What? - No!"

"Good place, just below the lock here. There's nowhere else for miles, and it'll be dark soon."

A pretty arched bridge spanned the point where the river left the canal and resumed its course between the woods and the water-meadows, and we tied up nearby. It was a lovely spot, - if one didn't look up.

Pete said he was bushed after steering all day, so I put a meal together, which we ate in near silence. The moment was coming for that Conversation, and then I'd have to spend the rest of the week with the guy.

"I think I'll go for a little walk before bed." I snatched my binoculars and fled.

The lock ahead was sinister in the twilight, a huge gate leaking water, so I went back the way we had come, over the bridge and beside the high wooded bank. The last of the sun was touching the tops of the trees. I wished I could be up there, instead of in this dark cutting.

And then I saw the steps cut into the slope, almost invisible and overgrown with ivy.

It was a steep climb, more of a ladder than a staircase, and I paused to get my breath at the top before venturing down the path that ran between the blackberry bushes. No one had been here for a long time. Rabbits scurried off as I moved, and trails of bramble blocked the way. I dodged an overhanging hawthorn branch, - and drew up short with a startled gasp.

For a second it really crossed my mind that the steps must have been one of those portals you read about in science fiction, and had transported me to another planet. I certainly seemed to have found a gap in the known world. Before me stretched a vast expanse of rocky nothingness, bounded, far on the other side, by a range of unnatural-looking cliffs, their strata layered as neatly as a textbook. In between was what one might have called a lake, if it hadn't been that unreal turquoise blue. It reminded me of a child's picture of the seaside, over-simplified and everything just wrong. Where there should have been seagulls swooping over golden sand, a pair of dismal black crows stood on a concrete-coloured shore.

This must be an old quarry, part of the cement works whose debris lay all around me, scattered amongst the stones and the flowers. - It was these that held me spellbound. Every rock-growing, waste-loving plant I could name, and one or two I couldn't, seemed to have made their home here. Wild strawberries and cinquefoil trailed across the broken glass and rotting plastic. Red centaury and golden St. John's wort had pushed their way through rusty wire and sheep-droppings. A cheerful white convolvulus twined in and out of an old tractor tyre, while every heap of rubble was crowned with spires of yellow mullein and delicate mignonette.

I shouldn't be here. The whole place reeked of danger. The ground was strewn with sharp rusty metal and lumps of jagged stone, and that green water was probably deep. Over to my left great struts were hanging from the half-demolished buildings, waiting to come crashing down in the slightest breeze. No doubt there was blue asbestos in that old silo. From what I could see, the owners had sensibly surrounded the site with a good strong fence to keep people out. They must have forgotten those steps up from the canal.

So why did I get the feeling that I wasn't alone here? That somebody else was in this derelict quarry, - someone who didn't cast a shadow, because my own was stretching right across the arena away from the setting sun. - Someone watching me, waiting to see where I went, what I did.

Ridiculous, of course. If anything I was all too alone up here. If I tripped and broke my ankle, or severed an artery on one of those bits of rusty metal, what were the chances of anyone discovering where I'd disappeared to? I must go back to the boat, right now. Better an argument with Pete than to risk spending the night, or endless nights, up here. Yet something made me reluctant to leave. It was so unearthly, like a weird dream, half magic, half nightmare. I knew I'd never get the chance to visit anywhere like this again.

What was that? A mewing sound. Not a cat, it came from the sky. A bird of prey of some kind, though it didn't look quite the right shape for a buzzard. I caught it with the binoculars and followed it to the chimney. Could it possibly be a peregrine, nesting in the top there among the weeds?

I lowered the glasses, - and almost jumped out of my skin. My instinct hadn't been wrong. A man was standing just a few yards away from me. Where the hell had he come from? We were right out in the open, and I hadn't heard him approach. He stood quite silently, gazing past me, with a vacant look that was frankly weird.

I felt a chill of fear. I was alone in this place with a weirdo. How fast could I run? He was dressed in khaki shorts and shirt like an old-fashioned scout master, - and then I spotted something else. He was wearing binoculars. The man was simply a bird-watcher, like me. If I could strike up a conversation, he'd probably turn out to be perfectly normal.

As always when nervous, I began to gabble. "Hi there, are you bird-watching too? Isn't this a wonderful place? I think there may be a peregrine nesting in that chimney, but you can't really be sure from here."

He looked at me then, and beckoned, before setting off towards the old buildings. I had the choice of turning tail and trying to find the way back to the steps before he caught me, or benefiting from the experience of a well-meaning nature-lover to see an interesting bird. I compromised by following at a safe distance. - Well, hardly safe in this obstacle course of twisted metal and concrete. I wondered how the man could get over the ground so lightly. No wonder he had crept up on me. He didn't seem to make a sound as he moved, or shift a single stone.

We had almost reached the chimney, and I was peering up eagerly to see if there was any sign of that nest, when suddenly he held up a hand to stop me. He pointed downwards. I looked where he indicated, and gave a horrified yelp.

In front of my feet was a gaping pit. I suppose it had once been a basement to one of the demolished buildings. Fronds of willow-herb and ragwort had grown round to disguise the edges. Fascinated, I stared down into the depths of what could so easily have been my grave. The brick-built walls were well-preserved and smooth. The small amount of debris that had collected at the bottom wasn't enough to climb up on. And once one had dropped the twenty odd feet into that prison, who would hear one's cries? It was a death-trap.

I glanced up to thank my fellow-birdwatcher for saving my life, but he had disappeared. I'd have to find my own way round the hole.

Somehow I still couldn't tear my gaze away. All kinds of strange things had fallen in down there, - pieces of concrete, a pile of khaki rags, and some long white sticks. ...No, those weren't sticks.

Pete's main concern seemed to be that I'd ruined the holiday. "It's so typical of you, Caro! If you hadn't insisted on trespassing somewhere you weren't supposed to be, no one would have even known it was there. We could have made it to Banbury, without all this fuss with the Police and stuff, and the wretched thing could have stayed buried in peace."

"Yes, but he wasn't buried, was he? - Or at peace?"

The sergeant who came to see me later said much the same thing. "You shouldn't have been there, of course. Bloody dangerous place. They've fenced those steps off now. On the other hand, it's closed a missing persons enquiry for us, - poor Tom Woodstock. A bit of a loner. Liked going off for long walks birdwatching. That's what he must have been doing, I suppose. He still had the binoculars round his neck."

The Lock Keeper

It was Jacko's idea to take a boat on the canal. "My cousin did that for his stag do. We had a brilliant time. - Go on," he urged us. "It'll be a laugh."

Jacko's ideas usually were, like the time we broke into the bus garage and painted them all in Bicester FC colours. Anyway, we usually did the things he said.

"We can take Charlie's boat," he told us. "He's on honeymoon. He'll never miss it."

So we set off from Aynho on the Friday afternoon.

Dazza had a mate in Oxford, so we headed in that direction. Apart from Jacko that time, none of us had ever been on a boat before, - hadn't even known the canal was there, to be honest.

Batesy had a bike, so we made him do the steering, but he said it wasn't at all the same as driving a Honda. Somehow the boat never seemed to go where you pointed the handle, and he'd crashed into a bridge, and rebounded into couple of cruisers before he started to get the hang of it. The trick was not to touch the steering thing at all. If you left it well alone, he discovered, it stayed more or less in the middle and the boat went more or less straight, - so long as the canal stayed straight, anyway.

But even when there weren't any bends or bridges or other boats to hold us up, our speed was rubbish. As Gary said, you could almost have walked to Oxford quicker, the pace we were going. But then Wayne found the throttle and set it to max, and that made it much more lively. All the boats on the bank rocked up and down like it was the sea, and some of the crusties who live on those things came out and shouted at us, and Wayne gave them the finger. It was mega.

Sly passed some cans round, and Macca got his radio out and turned it up full blast so we could hear it over the engine. We climbed onto the roof and started dancing about and hanging onto trees and stuff. Batesy complained he couldn't see where he was going, and we just laughed and told him to go to Specsavers, but then the canal went round a bend and Batesy didn't, and ended up with its nose stuck in the bank.

Everyone whistled and did cat-calls, and Batesy said "Get out and push, if you're so clever," and Dazza was so pissed he started climbing down the side. Before he could even get a leg in the water though, there was this huge hissing noise like a snake. - It was only a bloody great swan's nest! The damn bird went for him, hissing and spitting, and everyone knows they can break a man's arm with their wing. Shouldn't be allowed on the canal really. Luckily Macca found something heavy to throw at it, and the swan backed off.

Wayne picked up a long pole on the roof and had a go at shoving it into the bank, but it slipped into a hole where some ratty thing was living and put him off balance so he let go the end and it fell into the water. Still, he had pushed us off just enough to get moving again.

We were in the middle of nowhere, singing along to the radio, lobbing empty beer cans at the fishermen, and seeing who could throw a lighted fag onto the bank without it going out, when we spotted something strange, - there seemed to be a huge beam of wood right across the canal. As we got nearer, we found it was a gate, blocking the way so no one could get by. Batesy headed the nose in and we all jumped off and went to see what it was doing there and how to shift it. Turned out there was a kind of swimming-pool affair, with another gate at the far end, and a funny old house with a little garden.

We tried pulling and pushing at the gate, and Dazza climbed on the top and shook it, and Jacko gave it a kick for good measure, but the thing wouldn't budge. It rattled and creaked quite a bit, but it wasn't going to open for anybody.

And then this guy appeared out of the cottage. He was wearing a uniform with a peaked cap and looked sort of official. "Your first lock is it, lads?" he said. "Don't worry, I'm the lock-keeper. I'll help you through."

He told us we'd have to let a bit more water in before the gate would open. Trouble was, to do that it turned out you needed that bent bar with a hole in it - the one Macca had thrown at that swan.

"Never mind," he said, "I'll open the paddle. You lads get back on your boat."

We looked back and saw that wasn't going to be so easy. No one had thought to tie the rope on, and the boat was sliding out into the middle of the canal. Gary just managed to catch the end before it slipped off the bank and haul it in, and the others jumped aboard.

"No, you stay there, Craig," Jacko stopped me. "Then you can take hold of the rope again afterwards."

By that time the water was up to the top, and the lock-keeper showed me how to lean on the beam so the gate opened. Batesy's steering wasn't up to getting the boat into that narrow space, but Gary threw the rope over, and me and the lock-keeper pulled it in, while the others sang "Heave ho and up she rises!"

We shut the gate again behind them, and the lock-keeper went to open the paddle thingy in the other one so the water would go down again with the boat on top, - I was beginning to get the idea now.

"It'll take some time, lad," he had to shout above the radio. "This is the deepest lock on the whole system. You might as well hop back on board."

"Nah, wait a bit, Craig," Jacko advised, as I caught hold of the rail to heave myself up. "Let it go down a bit more and you'll be able to step straight onto the roof."

The boat was sinking down quite fast, like a lift between green wet walls. After a minute or so, I saw I'd better take my chance. "Make some room then, you guys!"

But by the time they'd shifted along to clear a space, the boat was already about ten feet below. "I ain't jumping that!" I called to them. "I'll wait till you've gone through, and get on after."

As the man had said, it took a long time. I watched the top of the boat going down...and down...and down. How deep was this thing supposed to be? The radio sounded odd in there, boom booming against the walls. Their voices, too, as they sank further and further into the darkness, - echoing and weird, like they'd turned into something strange and weren't really my mates at all.

After a while, I couldn't hear what they were saying. Then I couldn't even hear their voices.

"Hey!" An older guy in shorts had come up the steps beside the gate. "What's going on? Are you bringing a boat down, or can we take ours up?"

"Give us a chance mate. Can't you see we're just...?" I pointed to our own boat, - and found myself pointing at nothing. The lock was completely empty but for still, grey-green water, now not more than twelve feet below. Slime gleamed on the dark brickwork of the walls, and I could feel a chill rising from the depths which made me shiver. The gate at the other end swung a little, ready to open.

"Makes sense to take ours through first." The man went across to push on the beam. "Want to give me a hand?"

"But... But..." I heard myself clucking like a chicken.

He stared at me in surprise. "No point in resetting it empty, and wasting a lockful of water."

"But hang on, where's the...?" I looked all round, trying to make sense of what had happened. "There was this guy here," I stammered. "Called himself the lock keeper. He's done something funny with our boat."

The man shook his head. "Must have been having you on. They abolished lock keepers here years ago. It's a shame really," he added, as he finished opening the gate. "They always knew exactly how to deal with anyone on the canal who was being a bit of a nuisance."

The Living Dead

The engine gave a little cough, as if *Angelica* had got something caught in her throat, and then a more ominous splutter.

"Oh no, not now!" Rachel's fingers tightened round the tiller, urging her back to health by force of will.

But the boat was losing power. Another pathetic cough, and the engine cut out altogether. There was just enough way on her to make it to the bank. Rachel gave an anxious glance backwards before jumping off with the rope, but her view was cut off by a bend in the canal. Robert could be yards behind or miles.

She made fast to a hawthorn bush, risking blocking the towpath while she looked for mooring pins. No one was around to trip over the rope. In fact this seemed to be a particularly remote stretch of the canal. ...Oh why break down here, now? She and

Angelica had been doing so well. But she supposed it was asking a lot of a boat which had been laid up at its mooring for over a year to suddenly spring into life. There had been no chance to check things over, or start cleaning and preparing for a journey, without Robert wondering what the hell she was doing. As far as he was concerned *Angelica* was a place to store those of her possessions he didn't want to find room for on *Mother Gaia*. It had been difficult enough to find a moment to stow away what she needed, and extract a few stores she hoped he wouldn't miss.

Shortly after dawn this morning Rachel had slipped out of bed. She'd paused heart in mouth to confirm he was still sleeping, pulled on a minimum of clothes, and flown the few yards down the towpath. She'd cast off and bow-hauled *Angelica* to a safer distance before daring to start the engine, - and it *had* started, bless her.

How soon had Robert had woken and realised she hadn't just gone to the loo or out for some air? How long before he thought to glance down the towpath and saw *Angelica* missing? How much time had he wasted in anger and frustration, before setting off to fetch her back? She had no way of knowing.

It wasn't that she hadn't tried to talk to him, but Robert would always brush away the conversation with a "Nonsense!" and tell her she was just feeling down. He simply couldn't accept that they had made a mistake, or understand that what had once seemed quaint and romantic, Rachel now found impossibly stifling. Robert was happy with his reclusive, Spartan life, hidden away out of reach of TV signals and telephone masts, writing serious articles on green issues for obscure magazines which barely paid the cost of posting them, While she admired his commitment, Rachel had begun to realise that she couldn't exist that way herself, cut off from shops, and contact with other human beings, and the means to transport her paintings to somewhere she might have sold them. Withdrawing so totally from life had become all too close to being dead.

It was a long time since Rachel had worked a boat on her own, and slow going, but the same would apply to Robert. And a lot depended on luck with the lift-bridges and locks. Rachel had had the help of another boat going through the awkward Aynho Weir, but had to negotiate Nell Bridge on her own: mooring up, crossing that nightmare road to open the gate, nosing *Angelica* through the drain-like bridge, and climbing the slimy ladder so she could work the lock. Robert might have found all his bridges down and all the locks against him, or sailed through without a problem.

She knew what would happen if he succeeded in catching up with her. That was why she musn't, oh she *musn't* break down now! He would tell her how silly she was being, and point out how impossible it was for her to manage without him, and even though she knew it was more the other way round, - or perhaps because of that, Rachel would feel sorry for him, and he would finally guilt her into going back.

Now it looked as if that was to be precisely her fate. *Angelica* couldn't have chosen a more remote spot to give up the ghost, miles from a boatyard, or even a village with a garage. Thanks to Robert's antipathy to modern technology, she didn't even have a mobile phone.

With a sigh Rachel pulled up the heavy board which covered the engine, to see if there was anything obvious she herself could put right. It was hot to the touch, probably hotter than it should be, which made inspection difficult. Nothing had visibly broken off. ...Oh hell. To her shame, she felt a frustrated tear coursing down her cheek. She simply couldn't bear the thought of Robert turning up and finding her so blatantly demonstrating her inability to manage on her own. He would give one of his tolerant sighs, and repair the engine, explaining to her exactly how she had misused it, as if she would ever have the opportunity of doing so again. Then he would drag her back to that life that wasn't living.

"Want any help?"

Rachel jumped. She hadn't heard anyone coming along the towpath. In front of her was a young man with curly brown hair, warm brown eyes and a friendly smile. She smiled back, hoping he hadn't noticed that shameful tear.

"Poor *Angelica* seems to have died, and I've no idea what's wrong. I don't suppose you're any good with engines."

"Should be," he grinned. "I'm an engineer. Why don't I take a look?"

"It's still a bit hot," Rachel warned him, as he stepped aboard and looked down into the compartment. "Shall I see if I can find a cloth?"

"I'll be okay."

Indeed, he didn't seem to find it a problem, as he felt around the engine with what were clearly expert hands. "Might be a blocked filter. We'll have to take the cover off."

"Do you need any tools?" She tried to remember what she had.

"Nope. Carry them with me." For the first time she saw he'd left a toolbag on the path. He heaved it aboard and set to work.

Rachel could only watch and admire, - and not just the quiet efficiency with which he dismantled the engine. He had rolled up his sleeves to show strong brown arms, and his open-necked shirt revealed glimpses of a finely-toned chest. But there was more to make Rachel's heart skip than this man's gorgeous body. His 'can do' attitude, the swift competence with which he used his skill, gave him an attractive aura of vitality. Here was someone eager to engage with life, instead of treating it as something to be avoided.

"There, that should be okay now." He smiled up at her, and began to put his tools back in his bag.

"Oh, that's wonderful! Thank you so much. And I don't even know your name," she realised guiltily. "I'm Rachel."

"Nick. - Nick Sydenham."

"I can't believe how lucky I am that you were passing. I thought we were miles from anywhere."

He answered her unspoken question. "I'm working on the new road, just along there." He pointed further up the canal.

"A new road? I hadn't heard about that."

"Oh yes, it's going all the way up to Birmingham."

"Well, I don't see the news much," she admitted. "My partner doesn't believe in modern contraptions like television." She glanced behind at that bend in the canal.

"I'd better get back to work. I can see you're in a hurry."

"Can I give you a lift?" All at once she felt a great reluctance to lose his company.

"Oh, it's no distance." With a final wave, he set off up the towpath. Rachel concentrated on the business of unmooring, and by the time she was free to look up, he was already out of sight.

There was still no sign of Robert following, but even if he did catch up with her, Rachel realised she would never let him persuade her back with him now. Meeting someone so full of life and enthusiasm had made her see all the more clearly what a negative, deadening person Robert was. The canal ahead of her, leading into the unknown, represented all kinds of exciting possibilities for a new future. She and *Angelica* would settle in some cheerful spot, busy with holiday-makers, where she could start to earn a proper living from her painting. And the very first things she'd buy were a TV and a mobile phone.

She turned a corner and saw cars flying across the motorway bridge ahead. Strange to be in this peaceful world below, when everyone up there was in such a hurry. Robert would be appalled to hear there was going to be another new road. He still hadn't got over them building the M40 so close to the canal.

As she drew into its shadow, Rachel felt a little wave of sadness. Was it thinking about Robert, or the devastating effect of motorways on the countryside? Probably it was the sudden chill from the bridge which caused her to shiver on this sunny day.

And then something caught her eye, - a plaque in the wall. 'Dedicated to the memory of Nick Sydenham, a young engineer who died while helping to build this motorway'.

A Conflict of Personalities

We all agreed that there was something funny about Mr. Tarver. He seemed to keep his distance from the rest of the hotel-boat passengers in a most unfriendly way. He was gaunt and grey and pasty-looking, and spent a lot of time alone in his cabin, when the rest of us were helping Mac and Lindy with the locks, or getting together in the saloon for a drink and a gossip before dinner.

Mrs. Overthorpe couldn't stand him. As the nosiest of us, it infuriated her that Mr. Tarver never chatted, or revealed anything about himself.

"Who is this man?" she demanded one day, when he'd refused to answer questions about his job or his family or where he lived, and disappeared to his cabin again. "People shouldn't come on a hotel-boat holiday if they're not prepared to join in. I've a good mind to have a quiet word with Mac and Lindy. One doesn't like to cause trouble, but his sour face is spoiling it for the rest of us."

We all heard her 'quiet word'. In fact it was rather a loud one. "I've been coming on your boats for fourteen years," she reminded them, "and I've never met anybody quite so - well - strange. I really think you should ask him to leave. Someone like Mr. Tarver doesn't fit on *Crystal and Clara*."

Mac and Lindy were polite, as always, but even to please a regular client like Mrs. Overthorpe, they could hardly evict a passenger for the crime of looking gloomy.

And then at Cropredy things came to a head.

We'd been to explore the village, Mrs. Overthorpe leading the way as usual, showing off the sights of the place as if she owned it. We'd just come back to the boats and retired to change for dinner, when we heard an angry shriek.

"Are you haunting me or something?" Mrs. Overthorpe emerged red-faced, propelling Mr. Tarver in front of her. "I've just found this man in my cabin!"

She all but frog-marched him out onto the bank, - though he, it has to be said, looked as impassive as ever. "Call Mac and Lindy," she demanded.

I think poor Lindy was having a nap, but we fetched her out anyway, and Mac appeared from the engine compartment, wiping oily hands on a rag.

"As you know, I've never been one to complain," said Mrs. Overthorpe, "but when it comes to fellow passengers poking around among one's personal possessions... I insist that you send him packing. - Can't you see that you're not wanted here?" she turned on Mr. Tarver suddenly.

We were all a bit embarrassed. Mac and Lindy looked as if they weren't sure what to do.

"On the contrary," Mr. Tarver spoke for the first time, "I think you are the one who ought to leave."

"What do you mean?" Mrs. Overthorpe bridled. "I'm one of their oldest customers! I've been holidaying on *Crystal and Clara* ever since they began operating." She turned to Mac and Lindy for confirmation, and they nodded awkwardly.

"That's the trouble, isn't it," said Mr. Tarver. "You don't know when it's time to move on."

"Well of all the nerve!" Mrs. Overthorpe was purple with fury. "I've no intention of 'moving on', thank you very much. I'm perfectly happy where I am."

But then Mr. Tarver held up his hand, and declared in rather pompous tones: "I command you to depart and go to the place where you belong!"

And she went. - No, I don't mean she walked off in a huff; Mrs. Overthorpe literally disappeared. One minute she was there, puffing like an outraged turkey, the next she had vanished into thin air. Everyone was rather shocked. Only Mr. Tarver looked satisfied, as if he was enjoying his holiday at last.

And we were all surprised when Mac let out a huge sigh which sounded very much like relief. "Thank goodness for that! I never thought she'd really go."

"We simply couldn't get rid of her," Lindy explained to the rest of us. "Like she said, she came on our holidays every year, taking the whole thing over, and bossing the other passengers about. Mrs. Overthorpe was a pain in the neck even when she was alive, - but she died four years ago."

"We didn't realise what had happened till the bill came back with a solicitor's letter," said Mac. "And still she'd turn up every summer. In the end we had to call in Mr. Tarver."

Seeing us look him questioningly, Mr. Tarver finally revealed what he did. "I'm an investigator from the Paranormal Investigation Bureau, - I suppose you might call me a ghost-buster."

Landscape of Ghosts

The trees were casting the last of their leaves into the canal, and hedges that had been full of summer birdsong were bare and silent. The low sunlight threw long shadows across the empty fields, bringing the ridge and furrow of the ancient ploughlands into sharp relief. Only the chug of their engine broke the stillness, as it forged a path through that carpet of dead brown leaves.

"Isn't this great?" said Neil. "That's the good thing about coming so late in the season. We've got the canal to ourselves. It must be hours since we saw another boat."

Emma nodded, trying to view this remote spot as peaceful, rather than lonely. There weren't even any sheep or cattle to relieve the impression that every living thing had forsaken it. A solitary heron honked mournfully as he passed, as if anxious to escape as quickly as possible.

"Only problem is of course, it gets dark quickly. We'd better moor up soon," said Neil. "What about there?" Ahead was the derelict bridge of some long abandoned railway, its dark bricks smothered in creeper.

"Oh, I don't know. Can't we go on a bit?" Somehow Emma didn't like the thought of settling within the shadow of that brooding arch.

Neil misunderstood her. "Glad you're enjoying yourself," he grinned, "but we've got to stop some time. Nice and firm here for the mooring pins." He slowed the engine as he spoke, and turned the boat towards the bank. "Can you take the rope and jump off at the bow?"

"Right," he said with a satisfied stretch, when they were safely moored. "I could murder a bacon sandwich."

"No bread," Emma reminded him. "We finished it all for lunch."

"Oh hell!" Neil's face fell ludicrously. "I really fancied a bacon sarnie. - And what about breakfast? Can't have breakfast without toast and marmalade. We'll have to get some."

"Where from?" Emma asked him in amusement. "There aren't any shops round here."

"That last village we passed is bound to have one."

"Oh come on, that was miles back!"

Neil fetched the map, though it was too small-scale to show much detail. "There's this place," he pointed, "a bit further on."

"You can't tell how big it is," Emma objected, "or how far away. We've got potatoes. I'll do us some mash."

But once Neil had an idea in his head, there was no dislodging it. "I'll take the bike." He was already lifting it off the roof.

"Suppose I don't want to be left on my own?" She tried to smile.

"Oh, you'll be okay. Who's going to bother you out here?"

He sped off down the towpath almost before Emma could say goodbye. She only hoped he had some money with him.

She looked around her. One could say it was a beautiful spot to moor, far from any roads or other reminders of modern civilisation. That reedy inlet must be one of those abandoned loops, left to wind into nothingness when the canal was straightened in the early 19th century. It was somehow sad to think boats would never navigate up there again, just as those ridged fields would never hear the jingle of horses' harness or the shouts of a ploughboy. No more stream trains would chug across that bridge. Even the summer had gone. Emma felt as if she was the only warm thing left alive here, in this landscape of ghosts.

She shivered and went back inside. Might as well put the kettle on. It took ages to boil on that little gas flame, and Neil had said he wouldn't be long. She put up the table and got some plates out.

What was that? A sharp tap on the side of the boat. Emma jumped, then told herself not to be silly. It would be a branch or something tapping in the wind.

How long was 'not long'? Was it worth starting the bacon? She got the packet out of the fridge and put it all ready, but decided against lighting the grill. It wouldn't take a moment to cook once he was here.

Thump! Was that him? No, must be the wind again. - Except that it was a particularly calm day. One of the ropes flapping loose perhaps? Emma steeled herself to go and look. It might be something that needed dealing with.

But outside all was as still as ever. The ropes were coiled neatly round their stakes. No swans clustered round begging impatiently for food. No sign of a canoe which might have tapped the boat as it slipped by. Nothing wrong, - but nothing to explain that sound either.

Oh bother Neil for being so impulsive! They could easily have managed without bread. There were tins of spaghetti in the cupboard, or beans. But if he wanted something, it had to be now. That was why they had ended up on a boating trip so late in the year.

She could always phone him, of course. Relief flooded through her, as Emma realised she could find out exactly where Neil was and how long he was likely to be. She found her mobile and pressed the number, - but as so often, it was impossible to get a signal inside the steel boat. She took it outside, but that was no better. Too far from any masts, that was the trouble. Emma tried to rid herself of the feeling that such things hadn't been invented here.

The sun had almost set now. The bridge looked even spookier in outline, the ridged fields even bleaker and more deserted against the orange sky.

She went back inside and drew the curtains. In the sudden dimness, she noticed that her phone was printing out a text. - Funny, it hadn't beeped to say she had a message, and anyway she could have sworn she'd switched it off.

I'm coming to get you.

Neil, playing the fool, of course. Who did he think he was, Davina McCall? Still, it was good to be in contact. ...And then Emma saw something which made her breath catch: her mobile, over on the table where she had left it. This wasn't her phone, but Neil's.

She switched it off quickly, furious with him for leaving it behind, and frightening her with silly messages from his mates.

Then her own phone glowed from the table. She snatched it up, meaning to turn that off as well, but the message was brief enough to meet her unwilling eyes.

It won't be long.

Only the prospect of having to go outside again stopped Emma from hurling the thing into the canal.

Okay, long deep breaths. There was a logical explanation for what was happening here. Neil had realised he was missing his phone, and got someone else to ring the number in case it was somewhere nearby. And finding the signal problem, he'd sent a text instead, knowing Emma would see it. And then he'd tried her mobile as well. That made a kind of sense, didn't it?

So the next stage was for Emma to respond. She turned her phone back on, typed the one word *'Idiot'*, and looked for the previous caller's number. Strange, it didn't seem to be displayed, - only her sister's, who had rung last night.

Panicking a little, Emma tried ringing that. How wonderful it would be to hear Jan's voice out in the wilds here! Still no signal though. She switched it off in frustration.

Suddenly there was a violent hammering noise at the window. Not a knock, or a tap, but the sound of someone beating against the glass, determined to be let in. Emma gave a shriek of alarm, before realising that of course it was Neil back. ...Oh, thank heaven! She flung open the curtains.

But those weren't Neil's handsome, cheerful features pressed against the glass, a bare few inches away from her own. This was the face of an ugly old man, coarse and ill-shaven, showing broken teeth through lips which were parted in the lewdest, most evil grin Emma had ever seen.

With a scream which hurt her own ears, she snapped the curtains together, and cringed back to the far side of the cabin. Remembering the door, she seized all her courage and made a dash across to push the catch down and the two bolts home. After that, with no further to retreat in this small boat, she collapsed against the wall and gave way to uncontrollable sobs.

On the table beside her, the damn phone was glowing again.

Are you ready? I'm here.

Someone began to batter at the door.

It was a long time before she realised that between the blows she could hear Neil's voice, calling her name. "Emma! What's happened? Let me in."

Eventually she gathered enough strength to move to the door and unfasten it, but it was much longer before she could produce words to make any sense. At last Neil calmed her down enough to give him the gist of what had happened: the unexplained knocking, the text messages - there was no trace of them on either phone now - and that terrible, grinning face.

"Which window did you say it was?"

"That one," she pointed again with a trembling hand. The evil vision was burnt into her mind's eye.

"You must have imagined seeing a face then," Neil sounded almost relieved. "The towpath's *this* side, dummy! No one could possibly look through that window, unless he'd risen up out of the canal."

It was so nice to be in a pub, among cheerful, friendly people, with a log fire going, and a stiff drink in her hand. Emma had barely stopped shaking, even now.

"You were travelling late, weren't you?" remarked the landlord. "It was pitch dark when we saw you tie up."

"Yes, well, we had a perfectly good mooring back there by the old railway bridge," said Neil. "But old fussy-knickers here didn't fancy it, and insisted we moved on."

"By the old railway bridge, you say?" The man looked sympathetically at Emma. "Ah well, that's where old Roy Hargreaves had his cottage."

"We didn't see any houses," said Neil in surprise.

"No, it's not there now. They pulled it down shortly afterwards."

"After what?"

"After he was hanged for murder."

Emma couldn't help a little shriek.

"Yes, they knew how to deal with his sort in those days," the landlord observed grimly. "Roy was a very bad lot by all accounts, - a bit of a psycho. When one of the young boat-women disappeared near his cottage, Roy was strongly suspected of having something to do with it. Then another girl vanished, and the Police were called in. They found both of them buried in the garden." He paused to watch that sink in. Emma felt her spine go cold with horror.

"No, it's not a good place to stop overnight," he went on, "especially for young girls like yourself. The story goes that old Roy still gets his kicks by terrorising women, - especially if he finds the chance to catch them on their own."